AESOP'S FABLES

A CLASSIC ILLUSTRATED EDITION
AESOP'S FABLES

Compiled by
Russell Ash and Bernard Higton

PAVILION

First published in Great Britain in 1990 by
PAVILION BOOKS LIMITED
London House, Great Eastern Wharf,
Parkgate Road, London SW11 4NQ

Produced, edited and designed by Russell Ash and Bernard Higton
Introduction copyright © Russell Ash 1990
Designed by Bernard Higton

ISBN 1 85145 988 X

Printed and bound in Italy by New Interlitho

2 4 6 8 10 9 7 5 3

CONTENTS

Introduction 6

THE FABLES

Aesop and his Illustrators

BECAUSE early man lived in close proximity to animals, both the beasts he domesticated and those he hunted – as well as those that hunted him – it seems probable that animals appeared in the first stories he ever told. In many of those tales that have been handed down to us, the animals have human characteristics and convey simple moral lessons. Such stories are known as fables. They are found in ancient Egypt and India, but became known in the West principally from Greek sources, and it was in Greece, by the late fifth century BC, that Aesop came to be regarded as the greatest fable writer of all.

Heinrich Steinhöwel's image of Aesop (c.1476), adapted by Caxton and others in subsequent editions of 'Aesop's Fables'.

Who was Aesop? The Greek historian Herodotus tells us that he hailed from Phrygia and worked as a slave in the household of a family called Iadmon. Later writers embroidered these scanty details with the information that he was a cripple and had a speech impediment, that he was a favourite of King Croesus, and was put to death for blasphemy by the citizens of Delphi. Whether he ever existed is open to question, but the collected fables attributed to him have been told for over 2,500 years and have remained one of the most universally popular subjects during the five centuries that the illustrated book has existed.

Aesop's fables are generally short and humorous, conveying in down-to-earth language messages relating to the conduct of daily life, with modest warnings about loyalty, generosity and the virtue of hard work. The moral is often added as an afterthought, and does not always relate closely to the narrative that has gone before. While most fables feature animals, they are usually animals that behave like humans, satirically poking fun at human failings and revealing universal truths about human nature. Certain fables

The Wolf and the Crane from a 15th-century French manuscript.

Wenceslaus Hollar's detailed etching of The Crab and her Mother from a 1668 edition of 'Aesop's Fables'.

are so familiar that they have become clichés, and we now use such phrases as 'the Hare and the Tortoise' or 'the Boy who Cried Wolf' as a sort of symbolic shorthand. Sometimes the animals' ways are uniquely their own – the sly fox, the devious wolf and the proud lion – becoming components of our perception of the animal kingdom. We do not pause for a moment to marvel that the animals can speak to each other, the talking animals of Aesop being in certain respects the precursors of modern comic strips and cartoon films. In some fables the animals appear with humans, others are about people alone, and, in a few, classical Greek gods make an appearance, sitting in judgement over mortal men and creatures.

The earliest known written versions of Aesop's fables date from

the third century AD, and from then on they appear in innumerable Greek and Latin editions that were eventually translated into English, French and other languages. There is no definitive version – traditionally each writer retells his selection of fables, adapting them to suit his own style.

in the period before printed books, Aesop's fables were illustrated on ceramics, in medieval manuscripts and on textiles (including the eleventh-century Bayeux Tapestry, in which the fable of the Fox and the Crow appears in a border). Within a few years of the invention of printing, however, several illustrated versions of Aesop were published in Germany, Italy and Holland. The third English illustrated book ever printed, in 1484 by William Caxton, was an Aesop containing some 200 woodcuts, including a portrait of Aesop. During the subsequent 500 years, literally hundreds of editions of Aesop have been produced, their illustrations ranging from scrupulously drawn animals in detailed landscapes to crude sketches and from stylish works of decorative art to straightforward nursery pictures.

There was a long tradition of anonymous illustrators copying from one

King Log by Arthur Rackham (1912), an original drawing which he later enhanced with watercolour.

another until a few talented artists tackled the subject during the seventeenth century, among them Francis Barlow (1666) and Wenceslaus Hollar (1668). The work of both was much imitated during the next hundred years, but in the early nineteenth century new editions were published featuring woodcuts by the British artists Thomas Bewick (1818) and John Tenniel (1848), the original illustrator of *Alice in Wonderland*. Charles Henry Bennett's striking hand-coloured engravings (1857), depicting a cast of animal characters in fashionable Victorian costume, were followed a decade later by Ernest Henry Griset's large collection of sometimes macabre engravings (1869). Randolph Caldecott's fable illustrations for adults (1883) were accompanied by 'modern instances' to show their relevance to contemporary society, whereas Walter Crane aimed at a juvenile audience with his colourful *The Baby's Own Aesop* (1887), printed by the newly-invented technique of coloured photo-etching. He was succeeded by a number of illustrators working in a crisp Art Nouveau style, including Richard Heighway (1894), Charles Robinson (1895) and Percy J. Billinghurst (1899).

The memorable interpreters of Aesop in colour in the early years of this century include Edward Julius Detmold, who produced a range of stunning watercolours for a supremely elegant edition (1909), Charles James Folkard (1912) and Arthur Rackham, whose 1912 version is regarded as one of the finest ever published.

Alongside these, on both sides of the Atlantic, editions of Aesop were produced with caricature illustrations, while Edwin Noble in Great Britain (1914 and 1921) and Milo Winter in the United States (1919) applied a more conventional nursery book style which has been perpetuated by other artists up to the present day.

The earliest editions of Aesop were produced for adults rather than children. In the 1920s and 1930s the trend came full circle with various finely-printed books designed for grown-ups and to be kept away from sticky hands and scribbling crayons. Among the finest are those of the artists David Michael Jones (1928), Agnes Miller Parker (1931), Alexander Calder (1931) and Stephen Gooden (1936), beginning a tradition that continues with a magnificent series of Aesop prints by Edward Bawden.

The fables and illustrations that follow have been selected from the many hundreds of editions of *Aesop's Fables* published in Great Britain, Europe and the United States during the past 150 years. The pictures represent a broad cross-section of the work of some of the leading artists who have endeavoured to depict the fables, as well as some who may be less familiar. Together they exemplify the international appeal and visual diversity of what is one of the most popular literary subjects of all time.

THE FABLES

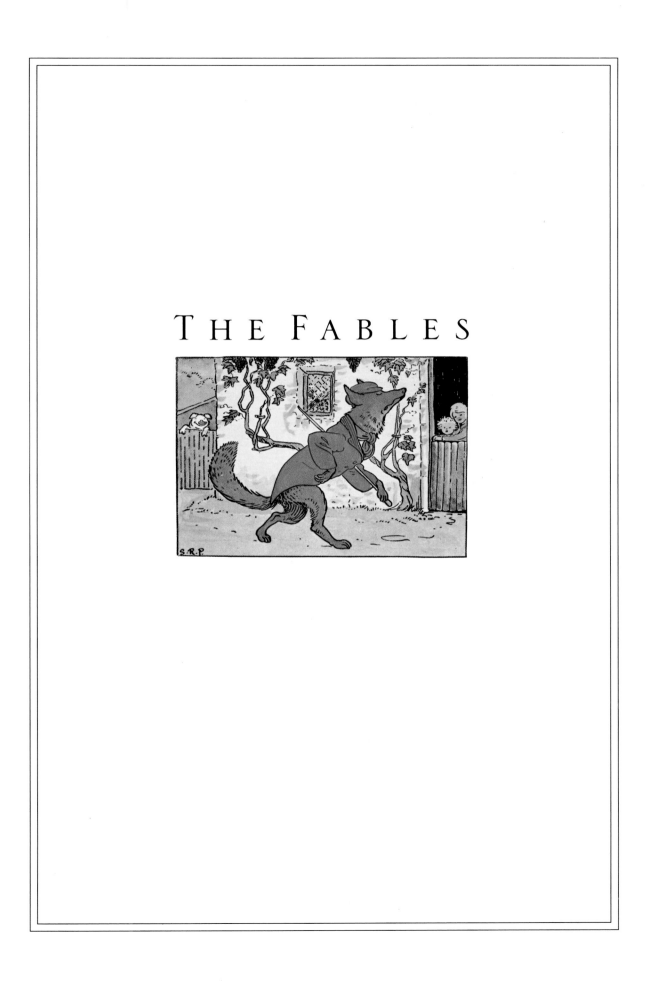

THE HARE AND THE TORTOISE

ONE day a hare was boasting of his running speed and laughing at the tortoise, for being so slow. Much to the hare's surprise the tortoise challenged him to a race. The hare, looking on the whole affair as a great joke, readily consented. The fox was selected to act as umpire, and hold the stakes. The race began and the hare, of course, soon left the tortoise far behind. Having reached the halfway point, and the day being warm, the hare decided to stop and play awhile. He then took a nap in a shady spot, thinking that if the tortoise passed him while he slept, he could easily overtake him before he reached the finish. The tortoise meanwhile plodded on, unwavering and unresting, straight toward his goal. The hare, however, slept longer than he intended, and when he woke up he was surprised to find that the tortoise was nowhere in sight. Off he went at full speed, but on reaching the finish-line, found that the tortoise was already there, waiting for his arrival.

Moral: Slow and steady wins the race.

ARTHUR RACKHAM

The Frog and the Ox

Many years ago there was a magnificent ox. One day, when he was taking an afternoon stroll, he attracted the attention of a drably dressed, thoroughly insignificant frog. Staring enviously at the splendid ox, the frog called out to his friends, "Look at the size of this fellow! He cuts a fine figure – but no finer than I could if I tried." With that he started to puff himself up, and quickly swelled to twice his normal size. "Am I now as big as our friend here?" he asked the other frogs; but they replied that he would have to do a great deal better than that. The frog puffed himself up some more, before asking the same question again. "No," said his friends this time, "and you had better stop trying or you will do yourself an injury." But the frog was so intent on emulating the ox that he went on puffing, and puffing, and puffing – till he burst.

Moral: Be true to your own character.

CHARLES HENRY BENNETT

THE WOLF AND THE CRANE

A WOLF devoured his prey so ravenously that a bone stuck in his throat, giving him great pain. He ran howling up and down, and offered to reward handsomely anyone who would pull it out. A crane, moved by pity as well as by the prospect of the money, undertook the dangerous task. Having removed the bone, he asked for the promised reward. "Reward!" cried the wolf. "Pray, you greedy fellow, what reward can you possibly require? You have had your head in my mouth, and instead of biting it off, I have let you pull it out unharmed. Count yourself lucky, you insolent bird, and don't ever again come within reach of my paw!"

Moral: Expect no gratitude if you show charity to an enemy.

RICHARD HEIGHWAY

ERNEST HENRY GRISET

THE MICE IN COUNCIL

ONCE upon a time the mice, feeling constantly in danger from a cat, resolved to call a meeting, to decide upon the best means of getting rid of this continual annoyance. Many plans were discussed and rejected. At last, a young mouse got up and proposed that a bell should be hung around the cat's neck, so that from then on they would always have advance warning of her coming, and so be able to escape. This proposition was hailed with the greatest applause, and unanimous agreement. Upon which an old mouse, who had sat silent all the while, got up and said that he considered the plan most ingenious, and that it would, no doubt, solve their problem. But he had one question to ask: Which one of them was going to put the bell around the cat's neck?

Moral: It is one thing to propose, and another to carry it out.

JACK ORR

EDWIN NOBLE

THE LION IN LOVE

A LION once fell in love with a woodman's daughter, and asked for her hand in marriage. The woodman was not much pleased with the offer, and declined the honour of so dangerous an alliance. When the lion became threatening, the man cunningly pretended to give in, saying: "I am honoured, sir. But what great teeth and claws you have – enough to frighten any girl! If you are to marry my daughter you must have your teeth drawn and your claws cut." The love-struck lion complied straight-away, and then called upon the father to accept him as a son-in-law. But the woodman, no longer afraid of the tamed and disarmed bully, seized a stout cudgel and drove him away.

Moral: Misfortune will surely befall him who loves unwisely.

THE·PEACOCK'S·COMPLAINT

THE Peacock con=
-sidered it wrong
That he had not the nightingale's
song;
So to Juno he went,
She replied, "Be content
With thy having, & hold thy
fool's tongue!"

·DO·NOT·QUARREL·WITH·NATURE·

The Peacock's Complaint

A PEACOCK was discontented with his ugly voice, and he went to the goddess Juno to complain about it. "It's true that you cannot sing," said the goddess, "but your great beauty more than makes up for it." But the peacock was not to be consoled. "What is the use of beauty," he asked, "with a voice like mine?" Now Juno grew impatient. "Each has his destined gift: you have beauty, the eagle strength, the nightingale song. Yet you alone are dissatisfied. Complain no more. If your present wish were granted, you would only find some other grievance."

Moral: Instead of envying the gifts of others, make the most of your own.

WALTER CRANE

THE COCK AND THE FOX

A COCK, perched among the branches of a lofty tree, crowed loudly. The shrillness of his voice echoed through the wood, and the well-known note brought a fox, who was prowling in quest of prey, to the spot. The fox, seeing the cock was at a great height, set his wits to work to find some way of bringing him down. He greeted the bird in his gentlest voice, and said, "Have you not heard, cousin, of the proclamation of universal peace and harmony among all kinds of beasts and birds? We are no longer to prey upon and devour one another, but love and friendship are to be the order of the day. Do come down, and we will talk over this great news at our leisure." The cock, who knew that the fox was only up to his old tricks, pretended to be watching something in the distance, and the fox asked him what it was he looked at so earnestly. "Why," said the cock, "I think I see a pack of hounds yonder." "Oh, then," said the fox, "I must be gone." "Why, cousin," said the cock; "pray do not go: I am just coming down. You are surely not afraid of dogs in these peaceable times!" "No, no," said the fox; "but they may not have heard of the proclamation yet!"

Moral: Beware sudden offers of friendship.

MILO WINTER

THE BEAR AND THE BEES

ABEAR happened on a fallen tree in which a swarm of bees had stored their honey. As he began to nose around, one of the swarm came home from the clover field. Guessing what the bear was after, the bee stung him sharply and then disappeared into the hollow log. The bear lost his temper and attacked the log with his claws, hoping to destroy the nest. But this brought out the whole swarm, and the bear had to take to his heels, and he was able to save himself only by diving into a pool.

Moral: It is wiser to bear a single injury in silence than to provoke a thousand by flying into a rage.

ERNEST HENRY GRISET

THE VAIN JACKDAW

JUPITER announced that he intended to appoint a king over the birds, and named a day on which they were to appear before his throne, when he would select the most beautiful of them all to be their ruler. Wishing to look their best for the occasion the birds went to the banks of a stream, where they busied themselves in washing and preening their feathers. The jackdaw was there along with the rest, and realized that, with his ugly plumage, he would have no chance of being chosen as he was; so he waited till they were all gone, and then picked up the most gaudy of the feathers they had dropped, and fastened them about his own body, with the result that he looked more magnificent than any of them. When the appointed day came, the birds assembled before Jupiter's throne; and, after inspecting them, he was about to make the jackdaw king, when all the rest set upon the king-elect, stripped him of his borrowed plumes, and exposed him for the jackdaw that he was.

Moral: Fine feathers do not make fine birds.

EDWARD JULIUS DETMOLD

THE WIND AND THE SUN

AN argument arose between the wind and the sun over which of them was the stronger. Noticing a traveller on his journey, they decided to put it to the test by seeing which of them could get the man's cloak off soonest. The wind began, sending a furious blast which nearly tore the cloak from its fastenings. But the

traveller seized the garment in both hands and clutched it to him so tightly that the wind went on blowing in vain till it was exhausted. The sun now had its turn, dispelling the clouds that had gathered and beaming its most sultry heat on the traveller's head. Soon growing faint from the heat, the man flung off his cloak and ran for the nearest shady place.

Moral: Persuasion is better than force.

CHARLES ROBINSON

THE TREES AND THE AXE

A WOODMAN came into a forest to ask the trees to give him a handle for his axe. It seemed such a modest request that the principal trees at once agreed to it, and it was decided that the plain homely ash should supply what was wanted. No sooner had the woodman got what he needed, than he began laying about him on all sides with his axe, felling the noblest trees in the forest. The oak, now seeing the whole matter too late, whispered to the cedar, "We should never have given in to the first request; if we had not sacrificed our humble neighbour, we might have yet stood for ages ourselves."

Moral: The betrayal of our friends may result in our own downfall.

ARTHUR RACKHAM

THE LION AND THE OTHER BEASTS

THE lion one day went out hunting with three other beasts, and they caught a stag. With the consent of the others, the lion divided it, cutting it into four equal portions; but when the others were about to take their shares, the lion stopped them, "Gently, my friends," he said. "The first of these portions is mine, as one of the party; the second also is mine, because of my rank among beasts; the third you will yield me as a tribute to my courage and nobleness of character; while, as to the fourth – why, if anyone wishes to dispute with me for it, let him begin, and we shall soon see whose it will be."

Moral: Never go into business with others without first agreeing how the profits will be shared.

THE MAN AND HIS TWO WIVES

A MAN whose hair was turning grey had two wives, one young and the other old. The elderly woman felt ashamed at being married to a man younger than herself, and made it a practice whenever he was with her to pick out all his black hairs; while the younger, anxious to conceal the fact that she had an elderly husband, used, similarly, to pull out the grey ones. So, between them, he was left without a hair on his head.

Moral: It is useless to try to outwit time.

THE TOWN MOUSE AND THE COUNTRY MOUSE

A COUNTRY mouse one day invited his friend from the town to come and visit him in the fields. On arrival the town mouse was depressed to find that dinner consisted of barleycorns and some earthy-tasting roots. "My poor friend," he exclaimed, "you live here like an ant! You must come and stay with me, and together we shall live off the fat of the land." So he took the country mouse back to the town with him, where he showed him a larder containing cheese, honey, oatmeal, figs and dates. The country mouse was amazed, and they sat down to enjoy a sumptuous meal. Scarcely had they begun, however, when the door of the larder opened and someone came in. The two mice ran off in alarm and hid themselves in the nearest uncomfortable hole. When all was quiet, they ventured out again, but then someone else came in and they had to scuttle away again. By now the visitor had had enough. "Goodbye," he said, "I'm off. I can see you live in the lap of luxury, but there's too much danger for my taste. I'm going home, where I can enjoy my simple dinner in peace."

Moral: A humble life with peace and quiet is better than a splendid one with danger and risk.

ARTHUR RACKHAM

CHARLES JAMES FOLKARD

THE FOX AND THE STORK

A FOX invited a stork to dinner. Deciding to play a trick on her, the fox served soup to his guest in a shallow dish. Of course, the fox was able to lap it up without difficulty, but the poor stork with her long beak could scarcely drink a drop, and she left the dinner as hungry as when she arrived. The fox pretended to be concerned, asking if perhaps the soup was not to the stork's liking. The stork made no comment, but offered to return her host's hospitality, inviting him to dinner the following day. The fox arrived and sat down, licking his lips in anticipation of the meal to come, but he was horrified when it was presented in a tall, narrow pitcher from which the stork could drink with ease, while he had to be content with licking the little that ran down the side. A hungry and wiser fox returned home, remarking to himself, "I can scarcely criticize my host for paying me back for my own unkind behaviour."

Moral: Do as you would be done by.

ARTHUR RACKHAM

EDWIN NOBLE

The Lion and the Mouse

A LION, tired from the chase, lay sleeping at full length under a shady tree. Some mice, scrambling over him while he slept, awoke him. Laying his paw upon one of them, he was about to crush him, but the mouse begged for mercy so plaintively that he let him go. Some time later, the lion was caught in a net laid by some hunters and, unable to free himself, made the forest rumble with his angry roars. The mouse whose life had been spared came and, with his sharp little teeth, gnawed through the ropes and set the lion free.

Moral: One good turn deserves another.

Little friends may prove great friends

Percy J. Billinghurst

THE OLD WOMAN AND HER MAIDS

A WIDOW, thrifty and industrious, had two servants whom she worked very hard. They were not allowed to lie long in bed in the mornings, for the old lady had them up at work as soon as the cock crowed. They hated having to get up at such an hour, especially in winter-time; and they thought that if it were not for the cock waking up their mistress so horribly early, they could sleep longer. So they caught it and wrung its neck. But they were not prepared for the consequences. For what happened was that their mistress, no longer having the cock's crowing to rely on as a timepiece, would wake them up earlier than ever, and set them to work in the middle of the night.

Moral: Too much cunning can have unfortunate results.

LUCY FITCH PERKINS

THE ASS AND THE LITTLE DOG

A MAN kept an ass and a little dog. The dog was well cared-for by his master, who played with him and let him lie on his lap, and whenever he went out to dinner he would return with some treat for him. The ass was also well provided for by his master, with a comfortable stable and plenty of oats and hay to eat, but in return he was expected to work grinding corn at the mill and to carry heavy loads from the field. When he compared his arduous life with the luxury and idleness enjoyed by the little dog he grew discontented with his lot. Thinking to himself that if he behaved like the dog he too might enjoy the same privileges, one day he broke free and entered his master's house, frisking about as he had seen the dog behave. However, being large and clumsy, all he succeeded in doing was to upset the table and smash the crockery, and when he tried to jump up on his master's lap, the servants feared for his life and beat the ass from the house with sticks. As he lay bruised in his stable he told himself, "I've got just what I deserved. Why couldn't I accept my natural position instead of trying to copy the antics of that little dog?"

Moral: It is foolish to attempt to be something one is not.

SOPHIA ROSAMOND PRAEGER

THE TWO PLAYMATES

IT happened once that a crane adopted a little orphaned tiger and brought him up with his own baby. They grew to be great friends, and, though they romped all day, no quarrels ever came up. In fact, gentler young ones never existed. One day another crane who was a bully, came along and handled the baby crane very roughly. The young crane called for help, and the tiger rushed up and gobbled up the bully in a trice, with perhaps the exception of a bone or two and a handful of feathers. The tiger had been brought up as a vegetarian, and this new morsel tickled his palate immensely. He licked his whiskers and winked slyly. "How I love you, little crane," he said, and in less time than it takes to tell of it, his playmate served as an excellent dessert to this unpremeditated meal.

Moral: What is bred in the bone will never out of the flesh.

JOSEPH J. MORA

THE CAT, THE COCK AND THE YOUNG MOUSE

A YOUNG mouse, returning to his mother after venturing out of his hole for the first time, said to her: "Mother, I came across two most remarkable creatures! One was beautiful and gentle, with velvety fur and a fine wavy tail; the other was a fearful monster. It had pieces of raw meat on its head and under its chin, which shook with every step it took. Suddenly it beat its sides and uttered such a dreadful cry that I fled in terror – just when I was about to talk to the kind-looking one." "Ah, my son," replied the mother, "your monster was just a harmless bird, but the other was a bloodthirsty cat, who would have eaten you in a moment."

Moral: Never trust outward appearances.

THE WOLF AND THE ASS

An ass was feeding when he saw a wolf lurking in the shadows. Knowing he was in danger, he thought of a plan to save himself. He pretended to be lame, and began to hobble painfully. When the wolf came up, the ass complained that he had stepped on a sharp thorn. "Please pull it out," he begged, groaning. "If you do not, it might stick in your throat when you eat me." The wolf did not wish to choke while eating his meal, so when the ass lifted his foot the wolf began to examine it carefully. Just then the ass kicked out with all his might, knocking the wolf over. As he got painfully to his feet, the ass galloped away to safety.

Moral: Beware of unexpected favours.

THE ANTS AND THE GRASSHOPPER

ONE fine winter day some ants were busy drying their store of corn, which had become rather damp during a long spell of rain. Presently up came a grasshopper and begged them to spare her a few grains. "For," she said, "I'm simply starving." The ants stopped work for a moment, though this was against their principles. "May we ask," said they, "what you were doing with yourself all last summer? Why didn't you collect a store of food for the winter?" "The fact is," replied the grasshopper, "I was so busy singing that I hadn't the time." "If you spent the summer singing," replied the ants, "you can't do better than spend the winter dancing." And they chuckled and went on with their work.

Moral: The idle get what they deserve.

EDWARD JULIUS DETMOLD

VENUS AND THE CAT

A CAT, having fallen in love with a young man, begged Venus to change her into a girl, in the hope of gaining his affections. The goddess, taking compassion on her weakness, transformed her into a beautiful maiden. The young man immediately fell in love with her, and soon they were married. One day Venus decided to see whether she had changed her habits as well as her form, and let a mouse run loose in the room where they were. The girl, forgetting her new condition, jumped up and ran to pounce on it, as if she wanted to eat it on the spot. On seeing this the goddess was so disgusted that she instantly turned her back into a cat.

Moral: One can change one's appearance but not one's nature.

ARTHUR RACKHAM

THE MOUNTAIN IN LABOUR

ANY years ago, a mighty rumbling was heard in a mountain. It was said to be in labour, and multitudes flocked together, from far and near, to see what it would produce. There was every kind of conjecture, from the wise and the ignorant alike. Days, weeks,

and finally months went by, as the rumbling grew gradually louder and the predictions of the experts grew ever wilder. Some said it would be the end of the world. Eventually the rumbling suddenly grew louder than ever, the mountain heaved and split open with a deafening roar, and everyone stood, transfixed, as out of the dust and noise there appeared – a mouse.

Moral: Magnificent promises are not always matched by performance.

RICHARD HEIGHWAY

THE FOX AND THE LION

A VERY young fox, who had never before seen a lion, happened to meet one in the forest. A single look was enough to send the fox off as fast as his legs would carry him to the nearest hiding place. The second time the fox saw the lion he stopped behind a tree to look at him for a moment before slinking away. But the third time, the fox went boldly up to the lion and, without turning a hair, slapped him on the back and said, "Hello there, old chap!"

Moral: Familiarity breeds contempt.

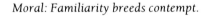

J. M. CONDÉ

THE CAT AND THE COCK

A CAT one day caught a cock, and resolved to make a meal of him, but first wanted to find a plausible excuse for killing the bird. She alleged that he made himself a nuisance to men by crowing at night and preventing them from sleeping. "Nay," answered the cock, "I only crow in the service of man," and he said he did men a good turn by waking them when it was time for them to start their day's work. "What nonsense you talk!" said the cat. "You are mistaken if you think that I'll be done out of my breakfast by an excuse like that," and she ate him.

Moral: An evil nature is bent on wrongdoing even when it hides behind the cloak of fairness.

The Bear and the Fox

Abear used to boast of his excessive love for man, saying that he never worried or mauled him when dead. The fox observed, with a smile, "I should have thought a lot more of your good nature if you never ate him alive."

Moral: Better to show mercy to the living than respect to the dead.

THE DOG IN THE MANGER

A DOG asleep in a manger full of hay was awakened by the cattle, which came in tired and hungry from working in the field. But the dog would not let them get near the manger, and snarled and snapped at their noses as if the manger were filled with the best meat and bones, all for himself. The cattle looked at the dog in disgust. "How selfish he is!" said one. "He cannot eat the hay, and yet he will not let us eat it who are so hungry for it!" Then the farmer came in. When he saw how the dog was acting, he seized a stick and drove him out of the stable, beating him for his unpleasant behaviour.

Moral: Do not grudge others what you cannot enjoy yourself.

EDWIN NOBLE

THE YOUNG MAN AND THE FICKLE WOMAN

A FICKLE woman said to a young man one day: "My dear, although there are many who love and desire me, I will love you alone, and I pray that you will be mine. I do not care about your wealth; all I want is you." And the young man, although he knew her to be fickle, replied: "Our minds are as one, for you are my heart's desire. It's true that you have deceived me in the past, but I adore you and I always will." And thus the trusting young man was beguiled by her.

Moral: Beware of those who insist they are not after your money.

The Fox and the Crow

ACROW was sitting on a branch of a tree with a piece of cheese in her beak when a fox saw her and thought hard about how he might get the cheese. Standing under the tree he looked up and said, "What a noble bird I see above me! Her beauty is without equal, the hue of her plumage exquisite. If only her voice is as sweet as her looks are fair, she ought without doubt to be Queen of the Birds." The crow was hugely flattered by this, and just to show the fox that she could sing she gave a loud "Caw!" Down came the cheese, of course, and the fox, snatching it up, said, "You have a voice, madam, I see. What you are sadly lacking is wits!"

Moral: Beware of flatterers.

THE MAN, HIS SON AND THE ASS

A MAN and his son were driving an ass to market, where it was to be sold. "Have you no more sense," said a passer-by, "than to trudge along, letting your ass go without a load?" So the man put his son on the ass, and they went on. "You lazy young rascal," said the next person they met; "aren't you ashamed to ride, and let your poor old father go on foot?" The man lifted off his son, and got on himself. Two women passed, one saying to the other, "Look at that selfish old fellow, riding while his little son follows on foot!" The man then took the boy up behind him. The next traveller they met asked the man whether the ass was his, and on being told that it was, he said, "No one would think so, from the way you use it. Why, you are better able to carry the ass than he is to carry both of you." So the man tied the ass's legs to a pole and, staggering under the weight, they carried it into the town. There they were greeted with so much laughter that the man, infuriated, threw the ass into the river and, seizing his son by the arm, set off home.

Moral: He who tries to please everybody pleases nobody.

ARTHUR RACKHAM

CHARLES JAMES FOLKARD

THE WOLF AND THE GOAT

A WOLF caught sight of a goat browsing above him on the scanty grass that was growing at the top of a precipitous rock and, being unable to get at her, tried to induce her to come lower down. "You are risking your life up there, madam, indeed you are," he called out in friendly fashion. "Pray take my advice and come down here, where you will find plenty of better food." But the goat was well accustomed to the tricks of the cunning wolf. "You don't care whether I eat good grass or bad," she replied. "What you want is to eat *me*!"

Moral: Beware of friendly advice from an enemy.

ARTHUR RACKHAM

THE PIPING FISHERMAN

A FISHERMAN, who cared more for his notes than his nets, seeing some fish in the sea, began playing on his pipe, thinking that they would jump out on shore. But finding himself disappointed, he took a casting-net, and caught a huge shoal of fish that he drew to land. When he saw the fish dancing and flapping about, he smiled and said, "Since you would not dance when I piped, I will have none of your dancing now."

Moral: It is a great art to do the right thing at the right time.

The Boys and the Frogs

SOME mischievous boys were playing on the edge of a pond, and, catching sight of some frogs swimming about in the shallow water, they began to amuse themselves by pelting them with stones, and killing several of them. At last one of the frogs put his head out of the water and said, "Oh, stop! stop! I beg of you: what is sport to you is death to us!"

Moral: We should not take our pleasures at others' expense.

THE FOX AND THE GRAPES

A FOX, feeling very hungry, made his way to a nearby vineyard, where he knew he would find a plentiful supply of grapes. The season had been a good one, and he licked his lips when he saw the huge bunches hanging from the vine. His joy was short-lived, however, for, try as he would, the grapes were just out of his reach. At last, tired by his vain efforts, he turned away in disgust, remarking: "Anyone who wants them may have them for me. They are too green and sour for my taste; I would not touch them even if they were given to me."

Moral: It is easy to despise what you cannot attain.

BORIS ARTZYBASHEFF

The Ass in the Lion's Skin

An ass found a lion's skin left in the forest by a hunter. He dressed himself in it, and amused himself by hiding in a thicket and rushing out suddenly at the animals who passed that way. All took to their heels the moment they saw him. The ass was so pleased to see the animals running away from him, just as if he were King Lion himself, that he could not keep from expressing his delight by a loud, harsh bray. A fox, who ran with the rest, stopped short as soon as he heard the voice, turned round and approached the ass, laughing: "If you had kept your mouth shut you might have frightened me, too. But you gave yourself away with that silly bray!"

Moral: A fool may deceive by his dress and appearance, but his words will soon show what he really is.

F. OPPER

THE DOG AND HIS SHADOW

A DOG, bearing in his mouth a piece of meat that he had stolen, was crossing a river on his way home when he saw his shadow reflected in the stream below. Thinking that it was another dog with another piece of meat, he snapped at it greedily to get this as well, but by opening his mouth merely dropped the piece that he had.

Moral: Greed begets nothing.

THE FOX AND THE MASK

A FOX one day stole into the house of an actor, and rummaging among a pile of stage properties he came across a beautifully fashioned mask. Touching it with his paw, he said, "What a handsome face we have here – a pity that it has no brains."

Moral: A fine appearance is a poor substitute for inner worth.

PHYLLIS A. TRERY

The Eagle and the Arrow

An eagle sat perched on a lofty rock, keeping a sharp look-out for prey. A huntsman, concealed in a cleft of the mountain and looking out for game, spied him there and shot an arrow at him. The shaft struck him full in the breast and pierced him through the heart. As the eagle lay in the agonies of death, he turned his eyes upon the arrow. "Ah, cruel fate!" he exclaimed. "That I should perish thus – but how much crueller still that the arrow which kills me should be winged with an eagle's feathers!"

Moral: Misfortunes to which we ourselves contribute are doubly bitter.

RICHARD HEIGHWAY

EDWARD JULIUS DETMOLD

THE COCK AND THE JEWEL

A BRISK young cock scratching in the dirt, happened to turn up a jewel. Feeling quite sure that it was something precious, but not knowing well what to do with it, he addressed it with an air of affected wisdom as follows: "You are a very fine thing, no doubt, but you are not at all to my taste. For my part, I would rather have one grain of delicious barley than all the jewels in the world."

Moral: What is precious to one may be worthless to another.

THE FROGS DESIRING A KING

THE frogs were grieved at their own lawless condition, so they asked the god Zeus to provide them with a king. Zeus, perceiving their simplicity, dropped a log of wood into the pool. At first the frogs were terrified by the splash and dived to the bottom. But after a while, seeing the log remain motionless, they climbed up and sat on it. Dissatisfied with their king, they went again to Zeus and begged him to give them a new ruler. By now Zeus was exasperated with them and sent them a stork, who gobbled them all up.

Moral: Know when to leave well enough alone.

CELIA M. FIENNES

THE GOOSE THAT LAID THE GOLDEN EGGS

A MAN and his wife had the good fortune to possess a goose which laid a golden egg every day. Lucky though they were, they soon began to think they were not getting rich fast enough, and, imagining the bird must be made of gold inside, they decided to kill it in order to secure the whole store of precious metal at once. But when they cut it open they found that it was just like any other goose. Thus, they neither got rich all at once, as they had hoped, nor enjoyed any longer the daily addition to their wealth.

Moral: Don't try to push your luck too far.

HARRY ROUNTREE

THE MONKEY AND THE DOLPHIN

WHEN people go on a voyage they often take with them lap-dogs or monkeys as pets to while away the time. So it was that a man returning to Athens from the East had a pet monkey on board with him. As they neared the coast of Attica a great storm burst upon them, and the ship capsized. All on board were thrown into the water, and tried to save themselves by swimming, the monkey among the rest. A dolphin saw him, and, supposing him to be a man, took him on his back and began swimming towards the shore. When they got near the Piraeus, which is the port of Athens, the dolphin asked the monkey if he was an Athenian. The monkey replied that he was, and added that he came of a very disting-uished family. "Then of course, you know the Piraeus," continued the dolphin. The monkey thought he was referring to some high official or other, and replied, "Oh, yes, he's a very old friend of mine." At that, detecting his hypocrisy, the dolphin was so disgusted that he dived below the surface, and the unfortunate monkey was quickly drowned.

Moral: Some people, ignorant of the truth, think they can make others swallow a pack of lies.

STEPHEN GOODEN

THE TRAVELLERS AND THE BEAR

ONE day two travellers came upon a bear. After the first had saved his skin by climbing a tree, the other, knowing he had no chance against the bear single-handed, threw himself on the ground and pretended to be dead. The bear came and sniffed around his ears but, thinking him to be dead, walked off. His friend asked, on descending from the tree, "What was the bear whispering in your ear?" "Oh, he just said I should think twice about travelling with people who run out on their friends."

Moral: Misfortune tests the sincerity of friendship.

THE THIEVES AND THE COCK

Some thieves once broke into a house, but found nothing in it worth carrying off but a cock. The poor cock said as much for himself as a cock could say, urging them to remember his services in crowing to get people up in time for their work. "Nay," said one of the thieves, "you had better say nothing about that. You alarm people and keep them waking, so that it is impossible for us to rob in comfort."

Moral: Even one's virtues will not find favour with everyone.

JACK ORR

THE ASTRONOMER

An astronomer used to go walking at night in order to gaze up at the stars. On one of his walks he absent-mindedly fell into a well. As he struggled to get out his cries for help attracted a passer-by who, on hearing what had happened, laughed and said, "My good sir, your efforts to peer into heaven have made you forget to look at what is under your feet!"

Moral: It is easy to overlook the obvious.

The Ass and his Driver

An ass that was being driven along the road bolted from his driver and, leaving the beaten track, made as fast as he could for the edge of a precipice. He was upon the point of falling over when his driver ran up and, seizing him by the tail, tried to pull him to safety. But the ass, resenting his driver's interference, pulled the opposite way, and the man was forced to let go. "Well, Jack," he said, "if you will be master, I cannot stop you."

Moral: A wilful beast must go his own way.

THE ROSE AND THE BUTTERFLY

A BUTTERFLY once fell in love with a beautiful rose. The rose was not indifferent, for the butterfly's wings were powdered in a charming pattern of gold and silver. And so, when he fluttered near and told how he loved her, she blushed rosily and agreed to be his sweetheart. After a long courtship and many whispered vows of constancy, the butterfly left his beloved. But alas! It was a long time before he came back to her. "Is this your constancy?" she exclaimed tearfully. "It is ages since you went away, and all the time you have been carrying on with all sorts of flowers. I saw you kiss Miss Geranium, and you fluttered around Miss Mignonette until Honey Bee chased you away. I wish he had stung you!" "Constancy!" laughed the butterfly. "I had no sooner left you than I saw Zephyr the wind kissing you. You carried on scandalously with Mr Bumble Bee and you made eyes at every single bug you could see. You can't expect any constancy from me!"

Moral: Do not expect others to be faithful unless you are faithful yourself.

MILO WINTER

THE BOY WHO CRIED WOLF

A SHEPHERD-BOY, who tended his flock not far from a village, used to amuse himself at times by crying out "Wolf! Wolf!" Two or three times his trick succeeded. The whole village came running out to his assistance; when all they got in return was to be laughed at for their pains. Then one day a wolf really came. The boy cried out in earnest, but his neighbours, supposing him to be at his old sport, paid no heed to his cries, and the wolf devoured the sheep.

Moral: Habitual liars are not believed even when they tell the truth.

THE KITE, THE HAWK AND
THE PIGEONS

SOME pigeons who were being persecuted by a kite employed a hawk as their protector. He set to work, but while pretending to carry out his new job, betrayed his employers' trust and seized more birds in two days than the kite could have done in twice as many months.

Moral: Be wary whom you trust.

THE HARES, THE FOXES AND THE EAGLES

THE hares were once engaged in a long and ferocious war with the eagles, which they saw little hope of winning without additional help. They therefore set about persuading the foxes to join them in an alliance against the eagles, and were delighted when the foxes replied most civilly that they would be glad to help them in any way they could. The hares' joy was short-lived, however, for the foxes went on to reveal, with no less sincerity, that they were on equally friendly terms with the eagles.

Moral: It is fruitless to form a partnership unless both partners have an equal commitment to the same cause.

THE LION AND THE GNAT

Lion was enraged by a gnat that was buzzing around his head, but the gnat was not in the least disturbed. "Do you think," he said spitefully, "that I am afraid of you because they call you king?" Then he flew at the lion and stung him sharply on the nose. In fury the lion struck at the gnat, but only succeeded in tearing himself with his claws. Again and again the gnat stung the lion, who was now roaring terribly. At last, worn out with rage and covered with wounds made by his own teeth and claws, the lion gave up the fight. The gnat buzzed away to tell the whole world about his victory, but instead flew straight into a spider's web. There, he who had defeated the king of beasts came to a miserable end, the prey of a little spider.

Moral: The least of our enemies is often the most to be feared.

EDWARD BAWDEN

THE LEOPARD AND THE FOX

A FOX and a leopard, resting lazily after a generous dinner, amused themselves by discussing their good looks. The leopard was very proud of his glossy, spotted coat and made disdainful remarks about the fox, whose appearance he declared was quite ordinary. The fox prided himself on his fine bushy tail with its tip of white, but he was wise enough to see that he could not rival the leopard in looks. Still he kept up a flow of sarcastic talk, just to exercise his wits and to have the fun of arguing. The leopard was about to lose his temper when the fox got up, yawning lazily. "You may have a very smart coat," he said, "but you would be a great deal better off if you had a little more smartness inside your head and less on your ribs, like me. That's what I call real beauty."

Moral: A fine coat is not always an indication of a fine mind.

ARNRID BANNIZA JOHNSTON

ILLUSTRATION SOURCES

Boris Artzybasheff, *Aesop's Fables* (1933) 69

Edward Bawden, unpublished *Aesop's Fables* lithographs (1970)
10 (top), 90, 91

Charles Henry Bennett, *The Fables of Aesop* (1857) 15

Percy J. Billinghurst, *A Hundred Fables of Aesop* (1899) 39

Randolph Caldecott, *Some of Aesop's Fables with Modern Instances* (1883) 32, 33

Alexander Calder, *Fables of Aesop* (1931) 10 (btm), 88, 89

J. M. Condé, *Aesop's Fables* (1909) 55

Walter Crane, *The Baby's Own Aesop* (1887) 2, 20, 21

Edward Julius Detmold, *The Fables of Aesop* (1909) 27, 49, 75

Celia M. Fiennes, *The Fables of Aesop* (1926) 76, 77, 96

Charles James Folkard, *Aesop's Fables* (1912) 35, 63

Stephen Gooden, *Aesop's Fables* (1936) 81

Ernest Henry Griset, *Aesop's Fables* (1869) 17, 25

Willi Harworth, *Ein Kalender für das Jahr 1933* (1932) 26, 67

Richard Heighway, *The Fables of Aesop* (1894) 16, 38, 50, 52, 53, 68, 74

Arnrid Banniza Johnston, *Fables from Aesop and Others* (1944) 93

David Michael Jones, *Aesop's Fables* (1928) 66

Joseph J. Mora, *The Animals of Aesop* (1901) 44, 45

Edwin Noble, *Aesop's Fables* (1914) 19; (1921) 37, 58, 59

F. Opper, *Aesop's Fables* (1916) 70, 71

Jack Orr, *Aesop's Fables* (1927) 18, 82, 83, 84, 85

Agnes Miller Parker, *The Fables of Aesop* (1931) 60, 61, 95

Lucy Fitch Perkins, *Aesop's Fables* (1908) 41

Sophia Rosamond Praeger, *Aesop's Fables* (1906) 11, 43

Arthur Rackham, *Aesop Fables* (1912) 3, 9, 12, 13, 22, 31, 34, 36, 42, 51, 54,
56, 57, 62, 64, 65, 80

Charles Robinson, *Aesop's Fables* (1895) 28, 29

Harry Rountree, *Aesop's Fables* (1934) 79

Phyllis A. Trery, *Aesop's Fables* (1925) 72, 73

Milo Winter, *The Aesop for Children* (1919) 23, 46, 47, 87

ACKNOWLEDGEMENTS

The editors and publishers wish to thank the following for
kindly granting permission to reproduce copyright illustrations
or permitting access to works in their collections:

ADAGP 10 (btm), 88, 89
Book Trust, London 93
Christie's Colour Library, 51
E.T. Archive 6
The Fine Art Society, London 10 (top), 90, 91
Fitzwilliam Museum, Cambridge 31
Gregynog Press 60, 61
Ian McPhail 27, 49, 75 (photo Sotheby's, London)
The Monotype Corporation Plc 66
The New York Public Library: Spencer Collection 9
D. Stempel AG 26, 67
Victoria & Albert Museum, London 26, 27, 66

All other illustrations are taken from editions of
Aesop's Fables and original drawings in private collections.

The valuable assistance of the following is gratefully
acknowledged:
Steve Dobell, Caroline Geary, James Hamilton, Anne Stevenson Hobbs,
Dee Jones, Ian McPhail, Peyton Skipwith